The warmth of the early morning summer sunshine caressed Ellie's legs as she lay on the lumpy, old bed. The shadows of the huge oak tree dappled the walls of the attic bedroom, even from as far away as the solid, old oak stood, but only at this time of day.

The tea, a little too milky and far too sweet, just the way Ellie liked it, stood on her dusty bedside table as she tried to muster up the energy to sit up and drink it. The bright yellow walls seemed just a little too bright as she squinted against the morning sunshine.

Sleep had totally evaded her as she had closed her eyes the night before. All the thoughts of the past few weeks flooded her mind and there was no escape from any of them.

It had all started on that unusually cold, summer evening, with that ear splitting scream at 3.30am. A scream that would have woken the dead, but Ellie feared the dead were already awake! Even after the scream had stopped, it still rung loud in Ellie's ears. But where had it come from and who or what had made that blood curdling noise?

Ellie shook Mark's arm. He was tall and muscley, just the touch of his thickset arms gave Ellie slightly more courage. He would have slept through an earthquake though, so it was no surprise that he had not heard it. He rolled towards her, slightly sluggish and bleary eyed, confusion etched on his face. But then, there it came again piercing the darkness. Mark shot up and looked at her.

"What the hell was that?"

She could see in his eyes that he was as scared as she was. Ellie was not sure whether to take comfort from that or not. She decided on the latter.

The light stung their eyes as Ellie flicked on the switch of the night light. They did not want to move, every fibre of their being pulling them away from that sound and away from danger but if someone had broke into their house, they sounded in trouble. So, they both slipped silently from the safety of the warm bed, grabbed their robes, and headed for the door.

The scream had sounded as though it had come from somewhere on the ground floor. The house was a large, old, three storeyed manor house and stood alone at the end of the lane. The nearest neighbour was a mile away so it couldn't have come from them. Maybe someone in distress had managed to break in, silently!

"Who are you trying to fool?"

Ellie chided herself for the stupid idea but was trying her hardest not to let the other, darker idea fester within her mind. That was way too terrifying!

Mark led them along the landing, their feet padding on the thick carpet, switching lights on as he edged his way forward, Ellie at his heels.

Ellie felt slightly reassured by the lights. She had seen way too many horror films and the lights always stopped working but now she was wishing those horror movie images would leave her alone. But still, the shadows played tricks in her mind and her nerves tingled through her body, her mouth dry and her heart pounding.

Only their bedroom was situated on the top floor of the house, so they started to descend the large, wooden staircase to the next landing below. Each stair creaked in an ominous way that Ellie had never noticed before, but she knew that was just the intensity of the situation rattling her nerves.

The window, halfway down the stairs, seemed to be watching their descent. Ellie half expected to see the image of a face peering at them through the stained glass. She couldn't shake the feeling that from somewhere they were being watched.

"This is not cool!" whispered Mark as they reached the first floor.

Again, the lights illuminated their path and spread into the shadows chasing away the darkness, giving it nowhere to hide. As they moved along the corridor, they pushed each door open, checking each room but each time the room came up empty.

They checked the large guest room, the bed looking stark and empty in the harsh light. The cushions on the bed sitting just where they always did. The highbacked chair sat tall and regal in the corner.

They looked into the smaller, spare room where one day Ellie hoped a crib would stand. It housed just a chair and a small bookshelf at present and both pieces of furniture looked lost in the room, small as it was. There were currently no curtains in the room and again Ellie had that awful feeling that a face would appear in the empty window, that feeling of being watched seemingly following her through the house.

They even checked the family bathroom and Ellie vowed never to leave the shower curtain drawn across again, her mind doing summersaults, along with her nerves, while she waited the few seconds it took for Mark to pull the curtain back revealing nothing but an empty bath. But what they hadn't noticed as they had searched was the small figure behind them, watching their progress through the house.

Everything was in its place and just where it should have been, so they continued down to the ground floor.

Nothing! No broken windows! The front and back door were still locked! Ellie's studio, with all her designs was, thankfully untouched and so too Mark's office. With no sign of a soul to be found anywhere, Mark looked at Ellie and frowned.

"Maybe we were both hearing things!" he said but he knew that that was just wishful thinking.

"Come on Mark, we both heard it. I heard it twice! That was shy I'd woken you. I don't know what it was but I sure as hell know it came from somewhere in this house."

"Well, you've seen what I've seen and so far, everything is in place, and no one appears to be here."

"I know!" Ellie said with a sigh. "I just can't shake the feeling that we are being watched.

They had lived in August House for three years. Mark had been promoted in his job as an editor and this meant they could finally afford to move to the area that Ellie and Mark had both always loved but only ever dreamed of.

August House had come onto the market almost instantly and they had seen it as a sign that this was to be the start of their dream come true. Everything happened so smoothly. Within weeks their flat had sold, and they had moved into the beautiful house on a sunny day in August. On that special day they had clearly seen why August House had got its name.

The light from the sun seemed to radiate through every door and window giving the house a magical, ethereal feel. The garden was long and had just one big, old oak tree standing sentinel at the foot while lush green lawns stretched out in front of it.

August House had not disappointed and during the three years that they had lived there, Mark and Ellie had been the happiest they had ever been. Even Mark's dream of becoming a writer had flourished and he had been able to leave the editing firm to concentrate on his passion. He had written three very successful stories and was on his way to becoming one of the most successful new writers of his generation.

Ellie was a textiles designer and August House had given her the space and renewed inspiration to work between her large studio at home and the pokey office in town. But in her bespoke studio her designs and creativity had blossomed, and the commissions had flooded in. Ellie's appointment book was full, and she too would soon be able to give up working for somebody else. She had waited so long for that opportunity.

They had even talked about starting a family as Ellie knew, with the help of a nanny, she would be able to work and be around to help raise a child. Could life get any better than this?

Ellie and Mark made sure that they had checked every inch of their home before finally returning to bed. They left all the lights ablaze, collapsed onto the lumpy old bed and clung to each other until the early morning light seeped into the room and they both finally fell back into a fitful slumber.

The next evening as Ellie and Mark sat in the comfort of the big settee, television on quietly, both absorbed in a documentary about snow leopards, they both looked at each other as the television switched off and they heard what could only be, the sound of small feet running down the stairs.

They waited in silent anticipation for the lounge door to be flung open and as they watched the door in mild terror, they saw the shadow pass in the small, illuminated gap at the bottom of the door. Silence followed. The television blared back into life momentarily then fell silent again and the air hung thick in the room.

 Mark stood, the waiting too much to bear, and pulled the door open sharply, expectantly. He did not know if he was relieved that the other side of the door stood empty or not. He knew what he had heard and seen, knew that Ellie had experienced exactly what he had, but what had they both just witnessed?

The next couple of nights passed without incident although Mark and Ellie still clung to each other as though their lives depended on it. On the third night their nerves finally seemed to be settling. Maybe it was the extra glass of wine with dinner or the warmth of the brandy at the end of the night, as it slid smoothly down, that helped them to both drop quickly and peacefully to sleep.

It was short lived.

The piercing scream was right beside them and Ellie screamed back into the darkness as Mark fumbled for the lights. Both of them expected to see someone standing at the foot of the bed but as soon as the light had flicked on, the screaming had abruptly stopped. No one had stood there, not a soul! Well not a soul that they could see, just their bedroom looking exactly as it had when they had dropped off to sleep.

Ellie started to sob.

"What's happening Mark?" she spluttered through the tears.

"I'm damned if I know," he said

"We must have done something wrong for this to be happening but what have we done. I just don't understand!"

What was happening to them and why now? They decided not to search the house that night. What was the point when the scream had happened right there beside them.

The following day Ellie and Mark decided that something had to be done. Something must have caused this disturbance in their beautiful home, and they couldn't sit back any longer just waiting for the next time for it to happen. If this carried on their lives would be shattered and it would all end in ruins.

They started their search at the public library. As they walked into the big, old, Gothic building they were met with the distinct, not unpleasant smell of old paper. The books lined the bookshelves and around the library people were sat in quiet contemplation, some deep into a book, transported into another world, while others were just sat, soaking in the peaceful atmosphere of the old building.

 Mark checked old newspaper cuttings, going back over many, many years, while Ellie looked for history books on the local area. They were looking for previous owners or any information on what the ground of August House might have been used for before the house had been built.

They drew a complete blank both at the library and at the local museum where they headed to, next. That had held no secrets for them either. Finally, after several hours they gave up their search, hungry, exhausted, and down hearted.

That night as Ellie slept, she was woken by gentle sobbing.

Her sobbing.

She lay awake for hours then, listening to the house creaking and groaning. She watched as the shadows danced across the walls and ceiling. There were no screams that night, but Ellie still had an immense feeling of foreboding as the birds in the garden started to sing their early morning ritual, welcoming the start of the new day ahead.

"I heard you last night Ellie," said Mark as he started slipping into his shirt and pulling on his trousers.

He splashed on his aftershave and straightened his tie in readiness for the meeting scheduled in town that morning and Ellie knew she would be left alone, without peace of mind from his presence and for a few hours longer than she felt she could cope with. Just a few minutes alone made her nerves jangle.

As Mark stood in front of the mirror, one final check of his appearance, he could see the worried look in Ellie's beautiful brown eyes and he felt guilty that he was having to leave her there alone. It was, unfortunately, a really important meeting that would help the sale of his next book if it all went to plan. He had done a lot of groundwork for this meeting to make sure everything would go accordingly and backing out at this late hour would be a catastrophic disaster. Eddie was a good man but not known for his patience.

"If I could postpone this meeting I would. You know it's a really important one and Eddie will not take too kindly to me backing out now."

"I know Mark. Don't worry about me."

But he did worry.

"Why don't you give Beth a call and have a catch up? Tell her what's been going on. Maybe she can think of a way to find out what's happening!"

"I might just do that, and we are well overdue a catch up. Thanks Mark. That's a great idea."

With that arranged Ellie busied herself getting ready. She showered, did her hair and makeup and even managed to eat some breakfast. In the light of day, the shadows slunk back and were absorbed and with her music gently filling the rooms Ellie didn't feel quite as wobbly as she had first predicted. She even left the house with a little spring in her step and her heart just a little lighter.

Beth and Ellie sat in the small, quaint, coffee shop, with its organza tablecloths and chipped teacups, and talked for hours over steaming hot lattes and thick, rich, hot chocolate fully loaded with whipped cream and marshmallows that melted down the side of the cup.

As soon as Beth had heard about the strange events that had happened at August House, she had been both mortified and terrified for her friend.

"You have got to be joking! How on earth can you sleep at night knowing that could happen at any minute and not knowing what's causing it?"

Beth sounded appalled but Ellie knew she meant well.

Beth and Ellie had known each other for almost thirty years. They had known each other before either of them could actually remember and had grown up to be more like sisters than friends. As children, they had always been in and out of each other's houses. They had attended the same primary school, St Jude's, had moved together up to Masefield Senior School and attended the same college, doing the same courses. They had partied together at university and continued to party when they had got home. Even when Mark had become an item, Ellie still made sure that Beth was securely in her life but there were often times when life got in the way as they had got older, and weeks could turn into months without getting together, but as soon as they were in each other's company the time would just melt away and Ellie knew that her and Beth would be friends for life.  She would definitely be partying on into the afterlife with this one!

The afterlife! Ellie had never really given much thought to the afterlife. Had never had reason to believe in ghosts, never really thought about what happened to you once you passed on, but now it felt like this might be where the answers lay.

"I'll call Jeremy as soon as I get back. He loves all of this kind of stuff so I know he will be able to help you. If not I'm sure he will know someone who will!" said Beth reassuringly.

Good old Jeremy. Ellie had often thought that Beth and Jeremy would become an item and eventually settle down. It had not worked out that way. They had however, always remained very close friends and Beth wouldn't have had it any other way.

"And he owes me a favour after I rescued him from that dodgy girl last year, pretending to be his disgruntled girlfriend!"

At this both Ellie and Beth had laughed. Beth had retold this story on several occasions both with and without Jeremy.

They hugged each other and Ellie headed for home feeling much better. She got back to August House, turned the key in the lock, pushed open the heavy oak door and froze.

Time stood totally still in those few seconds and the breath from Ellie's mouth could be seen billowing and twirling in the frosty air that suddenly surrounded her. Her heart hammered and even if she had wanted to scream, she felt that nothing would have escaped her mouth. Like a dream where you call out, but no sound escapes you or you try to run but make no ground.

There in the hallway was a sight that defied all laws of physics and rocked Ellie to her core. The six kitchen chairs, heavy oak kitchen chairs, were balanced on top of each other like artists in some freaky circus show. Each chair barely touching the one below it or to the side of it, each one almost seeming to float in the silence. Each one with only two legs seeming to hold it in place. Impossible, totally impossible but there and happening regardless.

Ellie, when she was eventually able to move, seemingly frozen to the spot for what felt like a lifetime, mesmerized by the sight that had affronted her, moved her hand up to her mouth and gasped. She knew Mark wouldn't have done this. This was beyond even his creative ability. However, his car wasn't on the drive so she knew he wasn't home and even if he had been home and left again, he just would not have been able to do this or have knowingly scared her in this way. Mark would never do anything to upset Ellie. That was not his way.

Ellie quickly shut the door and sat down heavy on the step, the coconut door mat prickling through her clothes but Ellie felt nothing except the extra fast beat of her heart and the fear coursing through her.

There was no way she was going to step foot back in that house without Mark. The hands on her watch seemed to be moving in slow motion as she waited. The sun dipped behind the clouds and Ellie sat shivering on the mat.

Cars trundled along the lane, each one offering a promise of rescue but none of them slowing at the end of her drive and hours seemed to pass.  Her hands were turning blue, and her bottom had started to go numb. Ellie might even have needed the toilet, but she had not noticed any of these things as she sat with her mind in turmoil.

Finally, the slowing of an engine signified the return of her husband and as the front of his car appeared between the large, wooden gate posts Ellie glimpsed the smile on Mark's face that told her his meeting had gone well.  She felt terrible when she saw the spark in his eyes, disappear in a blink as soon as he noticed her on the step and her resolve finally dissolved as he climbed out of the car.

By now big, round teardrops fell from Ellie's eyes and ran down her cheeks as she tried to explain what had happened and what was waiting for them on the other side of the door. Mark listened with incredulity. He was silently sure that Ellie must have been seeing things or her nerves had played tricks on her, but Ellie wasn't the sort of person to get easily, over emotional and had certainly never fabricated any situation or even stretched the truth in any way. It was her total honesty, amongst other things, that had made him fall so deeply in love with her.

It was now his turn to unlock the door and push it open. He too, stood on the threshold lost for words, surrounded by the frigid air. It was exactly as Ellie had described but seeing it was somehow worse.

Mark jumped as Ellie's cold fingers slid into his hand. He held her hand tightly as they made their way into the hallway and around the chairs. He needed the comfort of her hand as much as she needed his. As they walked in, they were both holding their breath without even realising.

August House stood silent, too silent. As they edged forward through the house, the chairs were not the only circus trick that was being performed. The kitchen cupboards all stood open, drawers pulled out and the knives and forks were all balancing on end, upon the long, oak table. They both let out a small cry at the sight that met their eyes.

Mark could feel Ellie's hand shaking within his as his heart hammered uncontrollably in his chest. Within seconds of them both seeing this spectacle, the cutlery crashed down deafeningly. It was as though something had been waiting for them to see it. They didn't see the flash of yellow behind the kitchen door or see the small shape of a child watching them in the shadows.

Ellie screamed as the cutlery came to rest and hung on to Mark even tighter at which point, he turned, dragging Ellie along behind him, back out of the house. This had suddenly got dangerous, very dangerous indeed. If something had the power to manifest that little spectacle, what was to stop them sending all that cutlery hurtling towards them or doing something even worse.

Mark was as livid as he was scared. How could he protect Ellie from a force as strong as that, that he could not even see? He slammed the front door shut behind them before jumping into the car. Mark threw the vehicle into reverse, just missed the gate posts, and swung out onto the lane before fleeing away from August House and everything he had just witnessed. His mind racing with what he had just seen and what they would do next.

With no luggage or belongings, they headed to the nearest hotel. They pulled into the hotel grounds and headed inside to the reception.

The hotel lobby was large, and the desk stretched up the entire side of the wall. Despite the size and openness of the entrance, the hotel still looked warm and inviting. They were both visibly shaken but the receptionist, while eyeing them with concern, carried out her duties without passing comment. She had seen far too many incidents with lovelorn couples to know not to get involved and knew that by the time they left the confines of the hotel room, everything would be just peachy again. Any rift would just melt away.

If only she knew.

This was no 'lover's quarrel' in need of healing.

In the room Ellie and Marked looked at each other and Ellie finally sighed knowing that at that moment at least, they were both safe. She started telling Mark about Jeremy. He had known Jeremy as long as Ellie had known Beth and knew that he believed in that kind of thing. The kind of thing that Mark would have called mumbo jumbo if he had not witnessed it first-hand. With no rational explanation, what else could it be?

They both jumped as Ellie's phone started to ring but Ellie just stood there looking at a picture of Jeremy, flashing on her screen. Eventually she answered and the flood gates broke.

"Jeremy we really need your help!" she sobbed. "You won't believe what just happened and I don't think…" Ellie didn't even pause to take a breath.

"Whoa Ellie, calm down and breath. I just spoke to Beth. She told me everything you guys are going through but you sound hysterical! Has something else happened? Is Mark with you?"

"Yes, he's here. And yes, so much more has happened."

Mark took the phone from Ellie's shaking hand. He relayed the events of the past couple of hours to Jeremy and Ellie could hear the long whistle coming from the phone as Mark continued to put him in the picture.

"Woah, bloody hell Mark! I'll be round in ten minutes."

"We can't go back there tonight mate; our nerves are totally shot. We are at The Johnson's Hotel for the night. We can meet you at August House first thing in the morning." The time was arranged, and Mark disconnected the call.

The evening was subdued, both deep in thought. But the food, hot bath and the good night sleep that followed, a sleep brought on from too much adrenalin having coursed through their veins, had enabled them to wake up more refreshed and with a little more resolve to get through the coming day.

Jeremy was waiting on the drive when Mark and Ellie got back to the house the next morning. It was raining and the clouds hung low and ominous above the house. The rain sounded like percussion as it dripped into flowerpots and bounced off the porch roof, but the silence flooded out of the house as soon as Mark opened the front door. Inside there was not a sound to be heard. Not even the pattering of the rain against the windows. The house looked unusually gloomy and not at all welcoming.

 The house was just saturated with an air of expectation. Jeremy visibly shuddered but not from the cold. He waited in the entrance to the house, staring amusingly at the chairs but there was no joy to be found in the sight that met his eyes.

He had heard about this kind of haunting but what Jeremy could not understand was why these things had started happening so out of the blue. He had been at the housewarming party so knew exactly how long Ellie and Mark had lived there and there had been no hint of anything like this before. Something had changed and he owed it to his friends to find out what. He only wished he knew how he was going to do that.

They made their way to the kitchen, the cutlery still lying silently on the kitchen table. He wished he had been a witness to that phenomenon, but nothing looked as though it was going to move anytime soon.

He was wrong.

The cupboard doors which had been silently stood open all banged shut at the same time making them all cry out. It wasn't even dark outside. He thought this kind of thing only happened during the night, not in broad daylight. Even with the dark clouds above, the house was usually still bright and airy although the atmosphere hung heavy and thick.

They quickly headed back out into the rain and stood staring at each other, each of them waiting and hoping for one of the others to come up with a solution or shout 'SURPRISE!'

But it didn't happen.

They were all lost for words as again, August House had delivered yet another chilling display.

There was, however, nothing for it but to return to the house and they headed back to the kitchen.

"Come on. Hiding out here in the rain isn't going to give us any answers."

Jeremy stood, waiting for Mark and Ellie to do the same.

"Just give me a minute," said Ellie Quietly

They were all feeling very unnerved as they headed back into the kitchen. It was a large, old-fashioned kitchen with a range on one wall and an open fire opposite. The cupboards lined the walls either side of the range and the large oak table stood in the middle of the room.

Mark picked up the poker iron that was resting in the hearth of the open fire. The fire was unlit, the grate clean and ready for the winter months to return. He wasn't sure what he was going to do with the poker but just the feel of the cold, heavy metal gripped in his hand made him feel safer, more in control. It was just then that they heard something. Something different.

It came from behind the wall next to the fireplace. Not behind the wall exactly, more like inside the wall. It was very quiet to begin with, just a slight scratching sound as though a small rodent had got trapped within the wall somehow. As the three of them stood looking at where the noise seemed to be seeping out of, it started to spread throughout the walls, and get louder and louder. It was not just coming from that small part of the wall anymore, but from every inch of every wall in the house and they covered their ears as the scratching sound became unbearable. Any minute now the walls would burst with a million rats scampering to be free.

It was unbearable and again they all ran for the front door, covering their ears as their feet took flight. As soon as the last foot had crossed the threshold the noise abruptly stopped! Jeremy looked at Ellie and Mark, deep concern etched across his handsome features.

"Bloody hell!" was all he managed to splutter as he stood trying to catch his breath and make sense of what had just happened to them.

"What the hell was that?"

Ellie let out a hysterical cackle of laughter. "That's exactly what Mark said!" Then she threw up.

The three of them sat on the front drive, mulling over what to do next. Ellie knew that somehow; they would have to go back in and confront whatever it was that was causing all this but wanted none of it. However, she loved her house so much that she knew something had to be done. However, what none of them realised was that once again, a small figure was watching them.

Jeremy was talking into his phone before Ellie had even realised, pulling her from her deep reverie and listened with a hint of renewed hope.

"Hey Mike, got a good one for you here mate. Are you and the boys free for an hour by any chance? This is your territory and I think you'll need to bring the big guns with you."

"Sounds like you have quite a problem there Jeremy. We will be over soon, and we will give you as long as you need."

"That's great mate, thanks."

Jeremy ended the call.

"Mike and the boys can be here in an hour so we might as well head to mine so that Ellie can clean up and have a drink."

"Thanks Jeremy, that sounds like a great idea. How does that sound to you, love?"

Ellie looked at Mark with those big, sad eyes and silently nodded. This was getting too much and as Mark looked at his wife, he suddenly realised that within the last few days she seemed to have diminished before his eyes, her face looking drawn and tight, her clothes just a little looser than they were usually. He was really concerned and really wanted answers.

Jeremy lived just a couple of minutes away. He messaged Mike and told him to let him know when they were at Autumn House, and they would come straight back around.

Ellie splashed cool, clear water over her face and used some of Jeremy's toothpaste to freshen her mouth with her finger. Not ideal but she was enormously grateful none the less. She hated being sick.

She joined the boys who were trying to drink a cup of tea but neither of them really wanted tea. A good stiff brandy would have been better, but Jeremy apologised for having no liquor in the house. At only ten in the morning, they persevered with the strong, hot, sweet tea that Jeremy had poured.

The van was being unloaded when Jeremy pulled back onto the drive. Cases of equipment and rolls of wires seemed to be everywhere. Monitors started to be carried in when the front door had been opened once the kitchen chairs had been returned to the right room.

It all looked rather excessive to Ellie, could not understand what most of the equipment would even be used for but as she didn't know anything about this kind of thing she just watched in silence, happy to let the boys do their stuff. As long as she got her beautiful house back and they got to the bottom of the problem she did not care.

The rooms were soon a hive of activity and Ellie sat quietly by Mark's desk which had been cleared of his writing work and was now housing two monitors, with a large, thick set, long haired bloke glued to the screens.

His walkie talkie crackled to life every so often but so far, he had nothing to impart. At least Ellie wasn't alone even though ponytail man had not said a word to her, and his broad bulk of a body gave her a little reassurance, even if it was against an enemy that they couldn't see. She watched Mark and Jeremy on one of the screens, trying to help but they looked as lost and as out of depth as she was feeling.

Mike stuck his head into the room.

"All set up now Ellie so hopefully we will get to see some of this activity you've been experiencing and help you get to the bottom of it."

He smiled at her as he left the room, momentarily giving her a little of the confidence that he was oozing. Why couldn't she be that laid back about it all, she wondered.

Two hours became three, became four, became five. Nothing. Not a squeaky door, not an open draw or a scream to be heard. The sound of the rats had vanished, and the eerie silence once more enveloped the house. Day turned into evening and the darkness descended.

Mark and Jeremy had joined her and ponytail man in Mark's office, the room that had been designated as the monitor room, quite early on in the investigation. They watched in silence as the rest of the crew walked around the house. There was no audio from the screens. The only voices to be heard were when the walkie talkie crackled to life, always making them jump and just a little more uneasy each time. They were watching the mouths of the investigators move between one another but had no idea of what was being called into the darkness. Ellie leaned on Mark's shoulder, the trauma of the day getting the better of her and with the sweet, safe smell of his body filling her nostrils and his strong arm around her shoulders, she fell asleep.

Mark was shaking her when she arose from that dream filled world. Her neck ached at the angle she had been sat at but that was soon forgotten as the quiet sound of scratching had started again and filled her head.

"I didn't want that awful noise to wake you and scare the living daylights out of you. I just thought if I woke you up now it would be less of a shock if it gets as loud as it did last time."

Ellie was touched by this small act of thoughtfulness and sought out Mark's hand in readiness for the crescendo that would undoubtedly follow. She was not to be disappointed as the noise level increased throughout the house and the sound of scratching rats amplified. Were they rats? This time it sounded like something much larger and along with that deafening sound came the menacing shadows running around the bottom of the walls and under the door frames.

Ellie instinctively pulled her feet up onto her chair and away from the black shadows even though there were no creatures to be seen. Ellie was taking no chances. Soon all the guys had joined her, each afraid of being touched by scurrying shadows. At that point Ellie put her hands firmly over her ears and closed her eyes tighter than she thought possible. In that instant she felt an icy cold hand touching her feet, felt the icy fingers as they dragged across the top of her skin, and she once more let out a piercing scream into the darkness.

The monitors all died instantly, and a deathly darkness filled the room. Ellie was shaking violently as Mark clung on to her. He should have left her at the hotel, but she didn't want to be alone. They sat in that room for a couple of hours, Ellie still with her eyes shut tight and Mark watching her dark shape surrounded by blackness, wishing he could do more to ease her terror. The scratching and the shadows had stopped as abruptly as they had started as soon as Ellie had felt those icy fingers, but the darkness seemed to seep into their very being and the horror of it all had rooted them there.

Even with all their experience and their high-tech equipment, Mike and his team had been unable to come up with any answers.

The light was starting to come up. Another day was dawning over August House and still there was no clue as to what was shattering their peaceful lives. The lads had to move on to another job in the next village and Ellie could only watch as the house was cleared of their equipment. Her heart was sinking even lower. How would they get to the bottom of this when the experts had been unable to find a reason behind it all? Who could help them now?

The gravel crunched as the battered, old van drove away. The sound of the engine getting fainter and fainter as it disappeared down the light dappled lane, the tall trees above waving their goodbye in the warm summer breeze and the events inside the house weighed heavily on Mark, Ellie, and Jeremy. At least the rain had stopped. Small consolation but a positive all the same.

Ellie stepped tentatively back through the front door noticing instantly, the icy temperature. That was not right. The sun, although early morning and high in the sky now, was still strong enough to have normally heated the house right through.

 She found Mark and Jeremy back in the kitchen. As soon as Ellie walked back into the room the faint scratching could be heard once more and Ellie's legs turned to jelly, she grabbed the nearest chair for support before the blackness that was engulfing her took her completely. Mark and Jeremy were quickly at her side, Mark once again with the poker in his hand and an increasingly worried look upon his face.

The noise remained just a faint sound this time. Not scuttling exactly, just gentle scratching but as quiet and as gentle as it was, it made your skin crawl and every hair on Mark's arms was standing on end, his neck prickling with fear and anxiety.

"It really sounds as though there is something stuck in the wall!"

Jeremy was pondering. He had always thought the wall next to the fireplace had looked odd, especially from outside. There was a part of wall on the outside of the house that did not match the contour of the wall on the inside.

"What is behind that wall?" He asked in bewilderment.

"I have no idea mate. What could be behind the wall but the garden and there are no shrubs planted there for mice or rats to be living amongst if that's what you were thinking!"

"No Mark. Have you never noticed how the outside wall juts out just there? It's not the chimney breast, that's further over."

At that Mark went out of the kitchen door that led out into the garden. In the three years that he had lived there, he never had noticed the brickwork, how it had been built about four feet upwards but then just stopped. Capped off with several bricks across the top. Why had Mark never noticed this? Ellie too, stood looking perplexed.

This part of the garden was not used very much. It was situated at the side of the house even though it was wide enough to be used as a stand-alone garden. It even got as much sun as the rest of the garden, but the loungers were all at the back of the house, watched over by the old, oak tree soldier, ready to offer shade on the hottest of days.

In this area there were no shrubs or bright colourful flowers in the borders. There were no borders even. The grass was kept short and tidy but that was as much use as the garden ever got. It was such a wasted space and Ellie made a mental note to fix that as soon as soon as this business was over. She only hoped that would be soon.

"I need to see what secret that brickwork is hiding!" said Mark, sounding braver than he was feeling.

Still armed with the poker he headed back into the kitchen. The gentle scratching was still audible, although none of them had noticed it from outside.

That was it, Mark just could not take any more and swung the poker with immense force at the exact area where the scratching was coming from. Jeremy and Ellie both jumped. A large scuff appeared on the wall, the scratching stopped and so, it felt, did Ellie's heart.

While Mark carried on his assault with the poker, Jeremy ran out to the shed and found a hammer. With as much gusto as he could muster after the long night that they had all just endured but being careful not to bludgeon Mark with the hammer, Jeremy too joined the smashing frenzy to get inside the wall.

They both stopped at precisely the same, exact moment. They both let out a small cry at exactly the same moment and Ellie felt herself craning her neck to get a better view of what the men had just seen. She gently pushed Mark's shoulder over so she could take a look.

 A large piece of plaster had finally given way and dropped to the floor, leaving a small hole. Dust was billowing from the smashed plaster and as the dust settled the hole became clearer and the sight that met Ellie's eyes she knew, would be a sight that would never leave her.

Small as it might have been, the hole was big enough for them all to see what was laying behind it. The end of a bony finger was protruding from the hole and seemed to point out at them accusingly.

What shocked them all was the size of that finger. It certainly had not belonged to an adult. The finger bones were too tiny and could only have belonged to a small child.

"Oh my God! I can't believe what I'm seeing!" muttered Ellie. "Who could do that to a child?"

Ellie was clutching at her stomach, a guttural instinct of a mother protecting her unborn baby. Mark and Jeremy carefully took down more of the concealing wall, brick by careful brick, and sure enough there was the skeleton of a small girl. They knew it was a girl because the threads of a little yellow dress were visible across the bones, and strands of her once long, blonde hair hung limply across her collar bone.

~

Eliza had lived in August house with her mother and father. She loved playing in the attic bedroom with her big doll's house and her spinning top. She had one teddy bear that used to sit opposite her while she poured pretend tea from the ornate, miniature tea set. This was her favourite game. Teddy would be one of the posh ladies that visited her mummy. One of the ladies that she was only ever allowed to see from the confines of her bedroom, peering down upon them from the small window at the front of the house. Watching as the feathers of their beautiful hats, fluttered in the breeze and their striking dresses flowed out behind them. They always made her mother look so dowdy in her dark grey dresses. Her mother did not think that married women should be seen out in public in such garish colours. Colours were for children on their Sunday visit to church or for the flowers in the garden, not respectable, married women.

But despite this Eliza loved her mother very dearly and most of all she enjoyed sitting with her mother while she read her stories. Her mother often made-up stories for her about Eliza and her bear. They would go to palaces and drink tea with kings and queens and Eliza would squeal with delight at the adventures bestowed upon her.

Her memories of her father were not so warm. Not because he had been a bad man, no not at all. But Eliza's father was very shy and although he would kiss his daughter goodnight every night without question, he rarely spoke to her during the times that he was at the house, with most of his time being spent at the local printing factory. He worked hard and as young as Eliza was, she knew that her daddy enabled her to have her beloved teddy bear and beautiful tea set while other children had nothing.

 She had rudely stared at some of those other children on the rare occasion that her mother had taken her to her father's factory. They would be huddled together on the pavement against a wall, their eyes too big and their rags, you couldn't call them clothes, had hung from their bony frames. Eliza knew that they had no mommy or daddy to give them a beautiful teddy bear or read them stories of kings and queens.

When Eliza was just six years old her whole world fell apart. A boy had come running onto the drive, shouting for her mother to come quickly. Eliza didn't know why and had stood frozen in the attic window as she had watched her mother's skirt tails disappear out of the gate.

Eliza had never been left alone before. She had stood at the window for an eternity before the vicar and her mother reappeared in the front of the house. Her mother looked to be crying, something Eliza had never seen before and from that day forward she had never seen her father again.

In a terrible accident at the factory her father had been crushed by the horse drawn cart, her mother deciding that Eliza was, in fact, too young to understand any of the events and decided that if she just didn't mention him again, Eliza would not have to suffer the heart ache that she was going through.

So that is how it was when a stranger showed up at the door, asking for work. He was a terrifying man and Eliza had been scared of him from the moment she had set eyes upon his scarred face. He had come, so her mother had told her, to do some of the jobs around the house that she could not do herself. Money was getting less and less by the day and her mother knew that soon the house would have to be sold. Her mother had only hoped that they would be able to get enough money to afford them a small cottage. Her biggest fear was having to knock on the door of the workhouse and reside there. Her mother had never been afraid to work but she knew that if that happened Eliza would be lost to her forever.

It was while that man had been working that something had happened to Eliza. She could not say exactly what had happened but from one moment of playing with her beloved teddy bear she suddenly found herself watching something that did not seem right.

The man was bricking up the large fireside seat that had been built into the wall next to the fireplace. She could see her favourite yellow dress and thought that she saw long blond hair just like hers. She couldn't find her mother anywhere. She had searched the house top to bottom, but her mother was nowhere to be found. Her teddy bear lay on the attic floor next to a broken cup and saucer from her tea set, but she could not even remember why she had stopped playing with them, let alone fathom where her mother had gone.

Before long the house had been emptied of all their lovely things and over time Eliza watched as different families with different children moved in and moved out. None of them ever saw Eliza, always standing in the shadows, staying out of the way. And this is how it had stayed until a warm sunny day in August.

Eliza had seen the moving truck pull onto the drive. She had recognised the couple who got out immediately. She had watched them as they had looked around her beautiful house and liked the smile on the lady's face and the caring touch as her husband led her from room to room, following a lady with a clipboard.

Something strange had happened though, when the couple moved a big old comfy bed into the attic and added a big window looking out over the back garden to her favourite tree. No one else had ever used her attic before unless it was to store junk. But Eliza had not minded. By now she had forgotten about her teddy, the tea set and her brightly coloured spinning top. Her days weren't as they used to be. She didn't change, had not got any taller or been given new and beautiful clothes to wear. Her yellow dress had faded but still fit her very well and her beautiful blonde hair still fell down past her shoulders. She had stopped calling out for her mother and could not even remember the last time she had eaten anything but then she never felt hungry or thirsty either.

One day she had quietly stood, unobserved, watching the lady in her special room. There were beautiful materials and colourful wallpapers around the room. Not hanging at the windows or covering the walls but everywhere around the room. There was a great big drawing board set up and the lady spent hours cutting samples of fabric, matching them to different pieces of wallpaper, sketching on large pieces of paper and writing down lots of different things. Here new rooms would come to life on the paper and Eliza knew that this woman loved doing this and soaked in the happy feelings that filled the room.

Before long Eliza noticed that the man would sit to a desk for hours upon hours, tapping at a flat box on the desktop. Sometimes he would read aloud the paragraph he had just completed, and Eliza would be transported back to a time of kings and queens but not sure why or where that memory had stirred from.

Eliza was happy in a way that she hadn't thought possible. She had been silently watching the comings and goings of August House for what had felt like an eternity, never leaving the grounds of the house, and often not even leaving the house itself for weeks, months, maybe even years at a time. The time span of Eliza being in this state was unclear to her, but one thing that was clear in her mind was that this couple had filled her house with beautiful things and an abundance of love.

Eliza found herself feeding off that love and watched them more and more, always unseen, and always from a distance. She knew she had felt this warmth and this love once before, but it had been so long ago that that part of her memory had completely faded away. The memory of the feeling however, had returned to her like a bolt out of the blue.

~

Ellie was heartbroken. In that instant she felt all the pain that the child's mother must have felt if she had known the fate of her precious little girl. Someone, somewhere in this world, all be it dead now, knew what they had done. Ellie shuddered that someone would have lived with this secret and, if it hadn't been the child's mother who killed her, her mother would have gone to her grave not knowing what had happened to the child or where her little girl had ended up.

The police were called, a forensic team swarmed the house and eventually the little skeleton was removed. The team were clear from the start that this was not something done in Ellie and Mark's lifetime.

Again, a search was made of the local history of the house and police data bases were searched across neighbouring villages too for any evidence or reports of local disappearances within the area, but they came up with a blank as to who this child was, as Ellie and Mark had drawn a blank during their search for information of the house and grounds.

After a week the police informed Mark and Ellie that although the search would continue, the child's body was going to be buried in a small grave in the local church, the vicar saying a prayer for her as she was interred. Mark, Ellie, Jeremy and Beth went to the little service, the vicar getting a little flustered as the child had no known name. Again, a small figure stood watching from the shadows.

"Why don't we call her August?"

 Mark smiled at his wife. Only Ellie would be so kind and thoughtful to come up with that. The service ended as Ellie lay a small posy of flowers on the little grave of freshly dug soil. As they turned away from the grave both Ellie and Mark caught a glimpse of yellow over by some bushes at the edge of the church yard. But as they both looked the image had gone. Neither of them said anything, both believing that their eyes had played tricks on them.

The next few days passed peacefully enough but Ellie was waking up each morning and being sick. She knew that shock could be the cause but that didn't really sit well with her.  And her suspicions had proved correct.

"We're having a baby!" she told Mark later that day. He hugged her tightly. Overwhelmed by the news.

"That's wonderful, so, so wonderful!"

~

Eliza had known. Eliza had felt a shift in her beautiful house even before the woman had realised. Although Eliza thought that there would always be enough love in that house for her to steal some of it, she did not feel that she could deprive the unborn child of even an ounce of that precious love. But while Eliza's secret was bricked up in that wall, she knew that she would never be able to leave that place. It had wracked her to the core of her soul, and she had screamed with all the energy she could muster. Eliza hadn't realised that her screams would be heard. She had moved silently through the walls and doors of the house, only ever observing, and never being seen, for such a long time that when the woman had shot up that first evening, she saw it as her chance to finally be discovered.

She had watched them as they had searched the house, looking for her but a part of her knew that this was going to have to be done carefully. She could not let them see her. If she did, Eliza knew that they would not look for her. She had no idea how she knew this, but some deep feeling within kept her moving in the shadows.

For several days Eliza had worked on how to get herself found, without being seen. It took real effort. The first two screams had really taken a lot of energy and it was a few days before she had any success again. The kitchen chairs had wiped her out totally but for some reason she had regained her strength just enough and just in time to work on the cutlery. When the couple had come into the kitchen, she had watched, invisibly, from behind the kitchen door as she'd made all the cutlery crash down to the table.

It wasn't until Eliza had seen the man pick up the poker that she knew what the outcome would be and how she would finish this once and for all. The day finally came when Eliza was able to watch as the man and his friend finally crashed and banged their way through the brick wall and Eliza saw her little yellow dress once more although now it was threadbare and only just visible within the dark and dusty hole in the wall.

As soon as her little skeleton had been removed from the premises, Eliza found that she was no longer tied to August house and its grounds. She was finally free and as she watched the little wooden box being lowered into the hole, Eliza felt an overwhelming love for the couple. She knew they had seen her as they had turned to go but she hadn't cared.

She had turned away from them and saw a figure in the distance that she thought she remembered. Eliza's mother had finally come back for her.

~

That night Ellie had had the strangest dream. The little girl had been talking to Ellie's tummy. She had no idea at the time, why or what the little girl had been saying. All she knew was that the little girl had been wearing a beautiful yellow dress and her blonde hair had hung down around her shoulders. Ellie had felt an immense feeling of love from this child and as she woke up, the stark realization of her situation, hit Ellie like a full-on hurricane.

Ellie sat bolt upright and looked at Mark.

"I know why the haunting took place." said Ellie with a sense of melancholy in her voice. She had felt devastated for that little girl when they had found her and even more so now that she knew there was a baby growing inside her.

"I think that once I became pregnant, August needed to be heard, needed to find her way home and I believe since we found her that she is now at peace."

Outside in the fresh, morning sunshine, a little girl in a bright yellow dress, her beautiful hair tied back with a matching ribbon, skipped along the lane holding her mummy's hand. As they turned the corner the sunlight blazed and the two walked off into the light. As they walked along their bodies became mere shadows dancing on the road and then they were gone.

The End


By

Sarah-Jane Brookes